S0-ECK-621

To

....

Love from,

Withdrawn from Collection

....

my first day of Kindergarten

Written by Louise Martin   Illustrated by Joanne Partis

sourcebooks
wonderland

Tomorrow, Kitten's off to school.
"It's going to be SO great.
Kindergarten... here I come.
I really cannot WAIT!

My family knows I'm good to go—
just look how much I've grown!
I brush my teeth and wash my paws,
and do things on my own."

The next day, Kitten starts to pack:
"But, Mama, I'll miss you!
What if I have butterflies?
I won't know what to do!"

"Kitten, you're so brave and kind,
ready for school to start.
No matter what, I'm here for you—
you're always in my heart."

Once outdoors, with backpack on,
Kitten feels SO big!
Mama takes a cute photo
as Kitten does a jig.

At the school, the teacher waves
and so does Kitten, too.
Mama snuggles Kitten tight
and whispers: "I love you!"

Outside the classroom, Kitten stops
and looks around in awe.
Then Kitten spots a shy classmate...
and lends a friendly paw.

When coats and backpacks (lunches, too)
are safely tucked away,
the classmates sing a welcome song
to celebrate their day.

Mr. Bear says: "Kindergarten's
going to be SO fun!
We'll play and learn and make new friends.
So, welcome everyone!"

Then Mr. Bear hands
out some jobs...

Today it is...

The

"Fox will find the day,

Mouse will draw the weather,

and Kitten will lead the way."

In art, while painting, Kitten wishes
Mama Cat was there.
Then, Kitten soon remembers
Mama's special words of care!

Later, when it's writing time,
Kitten's courage grows...
tracing letters, big and small,
with numbers in neat rows.

"I'll be just like my Mama
when she shows me how to write,
taking time to make my marks
the perfect size and height."

In music, Kitten learns a song,
and sings it loud and strong.
But Fox forgets the tune and sniffs:
"I think my beat is wrong."

Kitten says: "Don't worry, Fox.
I know just what to do.
We'll practice it together—
until you know it through and through."

They hum the tune while in the line...

then learn the words at lunch.

And pretty soon: "You've got it, Fox!"
"Oh, Kitten, thanks a bunch!"

Later, when the two go out,
they start to sing and play.

As others join in, Kitten cries:
"I'm having the BEST day!"

Back in class, Fox looks down.
He really misses Dad.
"I wish that he was here with me
to share the fun I've had."

Kitten smiles and says: "I know,
I miss my Mama, too.
But she's always in my heart,
the way your Dad's with you."

In science time, Bear makes a SPLASH!
"This is so much fun!
There's lots for us to see and learn,
until the day is done."

Then Mr. Bear says: "Time to dance!"
And all the class joins in.

Mouse shakes her tail, Fox jumps around,
and Kitten starts to spin!

It's time to go and Kitten cries:
"Kindergarten ROCKS!
Painting, writing, music, science,
and helping my friend, Fox."

Kitten leads the classmates out.
"Mama, I missed you!
But my first day was REALLY fun...
I can't wait for day two!"

Written by Louise Martin
Illustrated by Joanne Partis
Designed by Ryan Dunn

Copyright © Bidu Bidu Books Ltd 2023

Sourcebooks and the colophon are registered trademarks of Sourcebooks.
All rights reserved. No part of this book may be reproduced in any form or by
any electronic or mechanical means including information storage and retrieval
systems—except in the case of brief quotations embodied in critical articles or
reviews—without permission in writing from its publisher, Sourcebooks.

Published by Sourcebooks Wonderland,
an imprint of Sourcebooks Kids
P.O. Box 4410, Naperville, Illinois 60567-4410
(630) 961-3900
sourcebookskids.com

Source of Production: Guangzhou Great Dragon,
Conghua, Guangzhou, China
Date of Production: December 2022
Run Number: 5026130
Printed and bound in China
GD 10 9 8 7 6 5 4 3 2 1

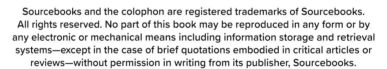
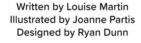

FSC
www.fsc.org

MIX
Paper | Supporting
responsible forestry
FSC® C117745

WELL DONE!

COMPLETED THE
FIRST DAY OF
KINDERGARTEN!

Stick your photo here

School: ....

Teacher: ....

Date: ....